MM

D0335702

Items should be returned on or before the last date
shown below. Items not already requested by other
borrowers may be renewed in person, in writing or by
telephone. To renew, please quote the number on the
barcode label. To renew online a PIN is required.
This can be requested at your local library.
Renew online @ **www.dublincitypubliclibraries.ie**
Fines charged for overdue items will include postage
incurred in recovery. Damage to or loss of items will
be charged to the borrower.

Leabharlanna Poiblí Chathair Bhaile Átha Cliath
Dublin City Public Libraries

Dublin City
Baile Átha Cliath

Date Due	Date Due	Date Due
06. FEB 13.		
28/10/14		

First published in 2008 in Great Britain by
Barrington Stoke Ltd
18 Walker St, Edinburgh, EH3 7LP

www.barringtonstoke.co.uk

ISBN: 978-1-84299-525-9

Printed in Great Britain by Bell & Bain Ltd

To Evelyne le Guern and a friendship that began with a letter in a bottle carried by the sea!

Contents

Story 1

The Drowned City of Ker-Is

1   Defeat   1

2   New Life for Old   3

3   A City by the Sea   9

4   Feasts, Games and Traps   14

5   The Red Prince   20

6   Drowned   25

7   "Have You Seen the Mermaid?"   33

Story 2

The Mermaid of Zennor

1   A Voice to Break a Heart   38

2   "Try to Please Your Father More!"   44

3   The Stranger's Eyes   47

4   "Don't Leave Us!"   53

5   Voices from the Sea   60

   A Final Word   64

   Battle Cards   66

The Drowned City of Ker-Is

Chapter 1
Defeat

A long time ago, King Gradlon of Cornwall grew rich from all the battles he had won. He owned a great fleet of boats. He led hundreds of young men out to sea. They fished for him and fought for him. They sailed his many boats into the cold north seas and made him very powerful.

As years passed, most of the young men grew tired of fighting. They had seen friends die in battle and longed for a different life.

They wanted to find wives, have children, and live in peace. But their king made them carry on.

One day, in the middle of a terrible winter, he ordered them to attack another fortress in the north. First one man rebelled. Then another, and another. The first boat turned around. Others followed. Soon every ship was sailing home, apart from the one carrying King Gradlon himself.

King Gradlon did not chase the men who left him. For the first time he felt alone and deeply depressed. After so many battles and adventures, he had been beaten. Not in battle, but by his own men.

Chapter 2
New Life for Old

Day and night, King Gradlon stayed alone, wrapped in his cloak, on the freezing deck of his ship. He hardly ate or spoke. The few loyal men who had stayed with him were scared and did not know what to do. They were out in the middle of an ice cold sea. Their nets were empty. Even the fish had fled away and they had no more food.

They might have died there. But one dark night, when King Gradlon felt that Death was near, he looked up and saw a woman standing above him. Her silver armour sparkled with stars. Her face was as pale as the moon, while her long red hair shone like the rising sun. King Gradlon held his breath. Was this not the Queen of the North who ruled a land forever frozen under snow? What was she doing here on his ship?

"I know you, King Gradlon," she said. "You are still young. I know your skill in battle. You are not like my husband, who is now old and rusty, like his sword."

She held out her hand. Her long white fingers reached down to him.

"Come with me! We shall get rid of my husband. Then I shall be your wife and return with you to your own land."

This was indeed the Queen! Her words stirred him. She was offering him a new life. King Gradlon rose up and took her hand.

"All hands on deck!" he shouted. "Pull up the anchor! We sail tonight."

A great cheer rose from his men. They could now break free from Death's icy fingers.

The Queen stood beside King Gradlon at the helm. She pointed the way north between floating islands of ice. At last they saw a great white castle through the freezing mist.

The Queen and King Gradlon stepped down into a little boat. They rowed towards the castle and landed below it. King Gradlon followed the Queen up narrow stairs to a bedroom, where they found the old King of the North sound asleep.

King Gradlon pulled out his sword. The Queen joined her hand with his. They held the sword above the old King of the North's heart. Then together they killed him.

Quickly, they filled a chest with gold.

"We shall take my magic horse," said the Queen. "You will soon see why I call him Morvarch, my 'Horse of the Sea'!"

At the sound of his name, a splendid horse appeared. His coat was black as night and fire blew from his nostrils. He shook his head and whinnied as King Gradlon lifted the Queen and the chest onto his back. Then King Gradlon leaped up.

Seconds later, they were galloping over the sea. Morvarch's hooves hardly touched the foam on the crests of the waves. Horse, King and Queen sped like the wind until they reached the King's boat.

They sailed south through the wild seas. They were near the Misty Isle when a storm struck. Violent winds and giant waves pushed their boat far away, back to the north and to the west. For one long year they were lost.

In that time, a baby girl was born to the Queen. They called her Dahut. But the Queen became very ill. With no doctor, nurse or medicine on the boat, she died.

Once again, King Gradlon fell into a terrible dark mood. But this time he had a baby to care for. If they did not reach land soon, the baby would die. He ordered his men to sail south until, at last, they saw rocks and reached a bay. King Gradlon gave thanks. He was even more thankful when he found that they could understand the language of the people. They had arrived in the land we call Brittany.

Chapter 3
A City by the Sea

King Gradlon loved his child. He adored her so much that he spent hours watching her play beside the sea. It was the place she liked best. Her golden hair danced in the breeze and she sang little songs to the sea as it lapped around her toes. As Princess Dahut grew into a beautiful young woman, she reminded him more and more of the Queen, her mother. Whatever his daughter asked for, King Gradlon gave it to her.

One day, Dahut said:

"Father, you have told me many times how my mother once lived in a fortress by the sea. I was born at sea, wasn't I? Will you build me a castle where I can hear the waves around me, day and night?"

So King Gradlon ordered his builders to come before him.

"I want you to draw plans for a great castle at the very edge of the sea," he told them. "It will be a fortress as large as a city. The water must lap at its walls but never flow over them."

When the plans were ready, King Gradlon asked his daughter to choose the one she liked best. Then carpenters, stone-masons, blacksmiths and all the other workers began to build Dahut's fortress city.

They began by making a huge wall of stone with a deep ditch all around it to keep the water out. There was only one gateway, with a bronze door that was bolted shut and locked with a silver key when the tide came in. Inside the great wall, they built the castle and many other buildings with domes and spires that soared into the sky. From far away it looked as if the city grew out of the sea itself.

When at last the work was finished, the builders presented the King with the silver key to the bronze door. King Gradlon turned to his daughter.

"This city is all yours, my dear Dahut," he said. "You may do as you wish here. I shall keep only this silver key on a chain around my neck. I alone shall open and close the gate-way to your city so the sea shall never harm us."

That night they held a feast inside the castle.

"What will you call your city?" Gradlon asked.

"Ker-Is," Dahut said with a laugh, "because it is like a 'Fortress of the Deep'."

Chapter 4
Feasts, Games and Traps

In the daytime, when the tide was out, King Gradlon left the bronze door open so that Princess Dahut could walk out along the sand. She was happy to spend hours sitting on a rock with a mirror, combing her long golden hair. She would sing to the sea.

I am yours, Ocean Blue

Born on your waves

Carried on your foam

I come from you!

Give me your ship-wrecks

Your gold, your jewels

Bring me your sailors

Fresh and new!

I am yours, Ocean Blue

Your treasures are mine

And mine are yours

I come from you!

Sailors passing in their boats would hear her song. One by one, the sailors landed and Dahut led them by the hand into the city. After each new sailor arrived with her, King Gradlon locked the bronze door behind them. They would enjoy themselves for the rest of the day and, in the evening, there was always a grand feast with music and dancing. While others were still dancing, Dahut would tie a jet-black mask around her sailor's eyes.

"Come, my friend! We have more games to play!" Dahut would laugh. Then she would lead him up the narrow steps to her room to carry on singing and dancing through the night.

But at sunrise, as soon as the early morning lark began to sing, the black mask on the sailor's face began to twist itself around his neck. No fingers could stop it! Slowly it squeezed out all the breath until the body fell limp.

Then Dahut would call her servant to take it away in secret on his horse to the Bay of the Dead. The young sailor's body was thrown back into the sea from where it had come.

This went on month after month, for many years. Each time a sailor's body was thrown into the sea, Ocean Blue would stir up a storm and a ship would be dashed against the rocks. The city of Ker-Is became rich on the treasure of these ship-wrecks.

News of Princess Dahut and her feasts spread far and wide. There was talk of sailors who went missing after attending her feasts. No one could say for sure what had happened to them. But as all the sailors were from other places, people in Ker-Is did no more than gossip.

However, an old monk called Saint Gwenole lived in an abbey a few miles away and he was furious at what he heard. He walked, with a bent back and a stick in each hand, to speak to her father.

"The Devil is surely at work!" the old monk warned. "Is it not strange how these young men vanish? What is more, the princess sets a bad example to others! How can you let her dance and play with young men so freely?"

King Gradlon listened and promised that he would talk to his strong-willed daughter. But he never did. Did he fear that she would leave him if he spoke harshly to her? As he grew older, it seemed that all he wanted was to see her forever laughing, forever happy.

Chapter 5
The Red Prince

One spring day, Dahut was about to walk by the sea, when a stranger rode up to her at the gate-way. The handsome stranger was dressed in blood-red from his cloak to his shoes. His horse's coat shone in the sun like polished grey steel. He had thin, pale hands and long nails. They were curved like the claws of a hawk.

"Welcome to Ker-Is," Dahut greeted him. She smiled, but he did not smile back. He did not even look at her as he steered his horse through the gate-way towards the castle in the heart of Ker-Is. He must be a prince!

For the first time, Dahut did not walk along the sea-shore and sing on her rock.

Instead she returned to her room and spent the day getting ready for the evening feast. She asked her father to make sure that the Red Prince, as she called him, would sit next to her. As ever, King Gradlon agreed to her wish.

All evening, Dahut spoke to their visitor. She told him about her mother, Queen of the North, and of her childhood by the sea. She told him many tales and legends. As she spoke she let him slip his long nails through her hair. It grew late. When King Gradlon's eyes were closing, he stood up slowly.

"I am no longer young like the two of you! I am ready for my bed."

The King smiled and wished his daughter and their visitor goodnight. He left the feasting hall. Everyone followed, apart from Dahut and the prince.

Now as the Red Prince began to whisper in her ear, a great rumble shook through the hall. Waves crashed against the walls of the fortress and the wind howled like a pack of wolves. Dahut placed her hand on the prince's arm.

"Have no fear," she said. "Let the wind and sea rage. Our walls are strong and the only key to our gate hangs from my father's neck."

"Does he not trust you with your own key?" The Red Prince looked into her eyes. His voice was smooth and sly. "Why should you not have it yourself? You would then be free to go in and out of your city when ever you wish."

"But I can take the key when ever I choose," Dahut boasted. "I shall take it from my father now while he is sleeping. Come and see for yourself!"

Chapter 6
Drowned

Dahut led the way to her father's bedroom and the Red Prince followed. King Gradlon lay fast asleep. His eyes flickered as if in a dream. Dahut held her breath as she leaned over the bed and lifted the silver key from the chain around his neck.

Immediately, there was an enormous roar as a wave higher than a mountain broke through the city walls. The Red Prince rushed to the window, shrieking with laughter as he leaped out.

Dahut froze with horror as King Gradlon woke up. He saw the key in his daughter's hand. In an instant, the King knew what she had done. They heard the devilish laughter drown in the sound of water crashing against the castle.

"Hurry, Father!" Dahut cried. "The wall has broken! Mother's horse Morvarch will help us flee!"

Dahut grabbed her father's hand. Together they rushed to the stables. Rising water swirled around them. King Gradlon leaped onto the horse. He was going to pull Dahut behind him when Morvarch reared up onto his back legs in the water.

"Help me, Father! Help me!" Dahut cried as the sea bubbled around her. She clutched on to the horse's back but the sea was dragging her down.

A sudden bolt of lightning lit up the dark sky.

"King Gradlon, leave your demon daughter!" a voice boomed.

A figure in a brown hood and cloak suddenly loomed in front of them above the foaming water. The face under the hood was as pale as a dead man's. Right away, King Gradlon knew that it was Saint Gwenole. The monk turned to Dahut.

"Shame on you!" The monk's voice shook. "You would betray your father and your city to the Devil himself."

"Oh, save me, Father!" cried Dahut. She felt herself slipping off the horse's back as the waves lashed her. She clutched at King Gradlon's fingers.

"Drop her!" ordered the monk. "She has broken your trust and done the Devil's work. She is not worthy of being saved."

A great wave rolled over them and Dahut felt her hands lose their grip as she was tossed off the horse's back. In her panic, she grabbed King Gradlon's leg. Her eyes pleaded with him. She might have pulled her father into the water beside her if King Gradlon hadn't put out his hand and pushed her down.

As the waves closed over Dahut's head, Ocean Blue dragged the princess down and claimed the city of Ker-Is. All of its people were drowned. Only King Gradlon was able to save himself as his horse swam on the crest of the waves and carried his master to the shore.

All night Morvarch galloped through forests, down valleys and over hills. All night King Gradlon battled with the nightmare in his head. All night, he heard the monk's words. *Leave your demon daughter!*

They rode until they reached a place where two rivers met between seven hills. The horse shone with sweat in the early morning sun.

"Halt!" cried Gradlon. "I will go no further!"

Morvarch stopped and the King climbed down. As soon as his feet touched the earth, he knew what he would do.

"To be betrayed by a daughter is a terrible thing," he said in a whisper. "But here, where I stand, I shall make a new city ... my own city. I shall put her out of my mind."

Chapter 7

"Have You Seen the Mermaid?"

Was it possible for King Gradlon to forget the daughter he had loved so much? You can go today to Brittany, to the place where he built his new city, which he called Quimper. There you can see between the high towers of its huge church, a stone statue of King Gradlon sitting on his horse. The people of the city placed the statue high up so that he could look down towards the drowned city by the sea. Perhaps they knew that he would never really forget the daughter that he had loved and drowned.

Ker-Is was not forgotten either. Some say that Paris got its name from 'Par-Is' because it wanted to be as beautiful as Ker-Is.

And Dahut? They say that she changed into a mermaid. Ask any fisherman in Brittany and he will sing you an old song ...

Fisherman, have you seen the mermaid

combing her hair

yellow as gold

in the afternoon sun

by the water's rim?

I have seen the mermaid

I have heard her sing

words as sad as the waves.

The Mermaid of Zennor

Chapter 1
A Voice to Break a Heart

Long, long ago, a mermaid swam into a bay on the north coast of Cornwall. From there she swam up a small stream. On the cliff above, the bells rang from the church tower in the little village of Zennor. It was evening and the bells were calling the villagers to church to pray for a safe night.

The mermaid peered up from beneath the water. Her dark hair flowed around her like a sea flower. She waited for the last person to make their way up the steep path and then up the steps into the church. Then she lifted her head above the water. As the church choir began to sing, she wriggled herself up onto a rock.

She loved to sing herself but now she was silent. Baby crabs and sea-shells clung to her long hair but she did not take out her mirror and comb. She sat as still as the rock itself.

One voice rang out clearly above all the others. Oh, it filled her with such joy! When the voice sang by itself, she thought her heart would burst. After the singing stopped, she could still hear that wonderful voice inside her head. For a while she sat, lost in the sound. It was lucky for her that it was dark when the villagers came out of the church. No one saw her slip back into the water.

Every evening, the mermaid returned to listen. Every evening she climbed onto a rock closer to the shore. The more she heard the wonderful voice, the more she longed for it. Its music was sweeter than anything she had heard in her own kingdom under the sea.

If you have made out that this was no ordinary mermaid, you are right. She was indeed Morveren, whose father was King of the Sea.

When Morveren could bear it no longer, she found her father in his cave.

"Father," she said, "I have heard the most beautiful voice in all the world. But it belongs to a creature on the land! Father, I must see who it is!"

"To hear is enough, my dear Morveren. To see is too much."

"Oh, Father," she cried. "The music has cast a spell on me. It is magic!"

"Not magic, Morveren." The King of the Sea shook his head. "It is only music from the mouth of a man."

"My heart will break with longing, Father. I will die down here if I cannot see the man who owns this voice." Her eyes filled with tears as large as pearls.

The King of the Sea could not bear to see his daughter cry.

"Go then," he said with a sigh, "but promise me that you will return by high tide. If you do not, you may never return. A mermaid cannot live in air for long."

So his daughter promised and the King gave her a dress that land women wear. It was a dress fit for a princess with pearls, coral, jade and many other jewels from the

sea. When she put it on, it covered her tail. Then she slipped a net over her long, dark hair.

She knew that her journey would not be easy. She would have to pull herself over the rocks, up the steep path of the cliff, and up the steps into the church. But she was not scared. The magic of the voice would make her strong.

"No one shall catch me, Father!" she laughed. "They shall not hook me like a herring!"

She waved goodbye and swam away towards the stream that would take her to the village of Zennor.

Chapter 2

"Try to Please Your Father More!"

Mathew Trewhella lived in a large farmhouse on a hill above Zennor. His mother and his friends called him 'Mathy'. His mother loved her tall, handsome son with his fine singing voice. Everyone said that Mathy was 'the apple of her eye'. When he was asked to sing solo in the church choir, she was so proud!

His father, however, always called him 'Mathew'. He often complained that his son was far too dreamy to be of help on the farm.

"Your mother goes on how you sing like an angel! But I say that you need to come down to earth!" he used to scold. "How will you ever manage a farm with your head stuck in the clouds?"

More than once, Mathy's father said he would send him out to sea with the lads from the fishermen's cottages.

"Our son doesn't know how lucky he is!" Mathy's father grumbled many times to his wife. "Those fisher lads would give their back teeth for the life he has."

At such times, Mathy's mother knew it was best not to say anything about their son's voice. Later she would talk to her son.

"You must try to please your father more, Mathy. He only wants the best for you. But you did sing like a bird at church last night!"

Chapter 3
The Stranger's Eyes

One fine spring evening, while he was singing the last hymn of the service, Mathy was surprised to see a new face at the back of the church. The young lady sat at the end of the pew nearest the door. Her eyes were fixed only on him and they shone so brightly that he almost forgot his words. Her dark hair was tied up with a net but the pearls around her neck glinted in the candle-light. Such beauty! Who could this stranger be?

He forced his eyes to turn away so he would not muddle his words. When he looked again, the young lady was gone.

He made up his mind to say nothing. Not even to his friends. Besides, everyone had been looking at their hymn books. No one had even turned their head to look at her. Perhaps he had just been dreaming!

But the next evening, as he sang the last hymn, he saw her again. She was in the same place in the pew nearest to the back door. Her eyes never left him. This time others noticed her too. Mathy saw them staring at her.

Yet by the end of the service she was gone. When he left the church, he looked up and down the road. Was there a carriage taking her away? But there was none.

Every evening in church, the stranger slipped in and later vanished. She never stayed for very long. She never talked with anyone and she always left before everyone else.

People began to gossip.

Everyone could see that the stranger had eyes only for Mathy. When his friends teased him, Mathy would just smile and quickly turn aside. How could he tell his friends how his heart jumped into his voice when the stranger's eyes met his?

Word got round to his father. When Mathy forgot to check that the chickens had been given their feed, his father told him off sharply.

"Don't think I haven't heard! A rich lady has her eye on you and there you are already dreaming of living in a castle! Well, dreams won't put meat on your table!"

Mathy knew not to answer back. He had never thought about whether the stranger was rich or whether she lived in a castle. All he could think about were her eyes and how they made his voice soar like a bird's.

Soon it was his mother's turn to try to talk with him about the stranger. But he did not want to hear her either.

"Oh, Mother," he protested. "I don't know who the lady is any more than you do. You know how people like to gossip and make up tales."

He saw that his words hurt his mother so he gave her a quick hug and made an excuse to hurry away.

So it went on. Every evening the strange lady slipped into the church and later vanished. The people of Zennor began to get used to her 'flitting', as they called it.

Mathy's father kept on grumbling about how his son always forgot to do things and his mother kept saying, "He'll come right!" As time went on, she pushed away her fears about the stranger.

Only Mathy felt the blaze of the stranger's eyes inside his heart. Only he knew how his heart was ready to burst. Only he knew the pain of being trapped forever. If the stranger always left before he finished singing his last verse, how would he ever get to know her?

Chapter 4
"Don't Leave Us!"

It was the evening service, one year after the strange lady had first come to the church. Mathy was about to begin singing the last hymn when she slipped through the door into the back pew. Mathy's heart leapt as he began to sing. His spirit flew up with the music.

Then suddenly he was not alone. He was no longer singing solo. Another voice had joined his! The stranger's voice rose up from the back of the church. Its wings touched his as their voices dipped and soared through the first and second verses. Heads turned. There was a murmuring. No one ever joined in with a solo!

Mathy's heart beat faster. If only these moments could last! If only they could sing these first two verses forever! He feared that the stranger would be gone, as always, by the time he reached the end of the third verse. A terrifying thought struck him as they began that third verse. Was she singing to say goodbye? But to his delight and amazement, the stranger's voice carried on. Their music wove together like that of two song-birds.

All this time, he hadn't dared to look at her. Now, as they began the fourth and final verse, his eyes met hers. Her eyes shone more brilliantly than ever! But the net over her hair was slipping! A mass of long wet gleaming hair fell down around her face. Her face and body suddenly seemed to be getting smaller.

Mathy's voice dried up. So did hers. He leaped from the choir stand. He ignored the gasps of his mother and the villagers as he rushed down towards her. She was facing the door but her hands gripped the pew as if she might fall.

"Stay!" he cried.

Great tears fell from her eyes. Mathy smelt the salt from the sea in her hair and tears.

"I cannot," she said in a whisper. "My breath is slipping from me."

"What can I do?" pleaded Mathy. She was beginning to shrivel up in front of his eyes.

"I have stayed too long. I must return home."

"Then let me help you!" said Mathy, sweeping her up into his arms.

A great "Oh!" swept through the church as her tail lifted up from beneath the hem of her skirt. Head swimming and heart pumping wildly, he pulled open the wooden door. Turning and pushing himself through, he carried his love with him.

For that is what she was. His love … and he was hers. Why else would she have risked her life to come out of the sea every evening to hear – to see – him sing? He knew what the old tales said. Mermaids cannot breathe in air like humans. Stay too long and they die.

Mathy ran with his mermaid in his arms. His long strides carried them across the village towards the path that led to the cliff. He heard the shouts and yells behind him.

Above them all, he heard his mother's cries.

"Don't go, Mathy! Don't leave us, Mathy! Come back, my son! Don't go!"

But his love was dying in his arms and he had to reach the water. Down, down the cliff path he stumbled. Through the bracken and brambles. Between boulders, over rocks, across the wet sand of the beach. The tide was sweeping out. His shoes were wet. Waves slapped his ankles, pulled at his trousers, tugged at his coat.

The arms of his love were around his neck. Their hearts beat together, their breath joined as one. How could he let her go? The waters closed over them.

Chapter 5
Voices From the Sea

No one ever saw Mathy again.

But this is not the end of the story. A little while after Mathy and the mermaid vanished, some fishermen from Zennor came back from fishing in the bay with a strange tale. They had heard singing under the water at the same time as the church bells were ringing from the cliff top. They swore that the voice sounded just like Mathy's.

At first the villagers didn't believe them. But then other fishermen came back with the same story and others too. So, in the end, they told Mathy's parents. Every fisherman said that the voice was so fine and pure that it gave him hope for the night ahead.

This gave his mother some comfort. She often spoke of Mathy and his 'angel voice'. She would not speak of the mermaid but in her heart she called her "That sea creature that stole my son."

Mathy's father turned more and more inward and silent. The poor man had never understood Mathy. He had wanted a son to share his farm and his love of his land. Perhaps deep down he felt that he had never really had a son.

****

Some years later, the boys who had been fisher lads when Mathy was a young dreamer were now grown up, with children of their own. Late one afternoon, two of them were fishing off the coast of Zennor. As the sun was going down, they dropped anchor. They were surprised by a voice. It sounded like a woman but they were too far out for someone to be calling from the land. The voice came from the side of the setting sun. They looked over-board and were amazed by what they saw. After rowing back to land, they were bursting to tell the people of Zennor.

"It was that mermaid that took Mathy Trewhella!"

"She swam up to us!"

"No! You're just making things up!" the villagers protested. "The sun was in your eyes!"

"She spoke to us! We swear!"

"She said, 'Would you kindly move your anchor! It's blocking our door. I need to get in to Mathy and the children!'"

The fishermen looked at each other and nodded.

"That's the honest truth!" said one.

"Why ever would we make up such a story?" added the other, and that was that.

A Final Word

My dad told me this story when I was a child in South Africa. He was very musical, like Mathy, and our surname was 'Trewhela'. With a twinkle in his eye, he told me that Mathy and the Mermaid of Zennor were our Cornish ancestors. When I asked for proof, he pointed to our *very, very* narrow feet and ankles!

Barrington Stoke would like to thank all its readers
for commenting on the manuscript before
publication and in particular:

Caitlin Allison

Aimee Armstrong

Scott Bain

Kieran Dalziell

Conor Davidson

Natalie Ewing

Lynzi Heavey

Amy Stilwell

Amie Trainor

Mrs Walker

Become a Consultant!

Would you like to give us feedback on our titles before
they are published? Contact us at the email address
below – we'd love to hear from you!

info@barringtonstoke.co.uk
www.barringtonstoke.co.uk

BATTLE CARDS

Beverley Naidoo

Author

Favourite hero:
The little African hare. He plays tricks on bigger, bossier animals who think that big is best.

Favourite monster:
The tick-tock crocodile in Peter Pan.

Special secret power:
A secret is a secret. (When I was a child, I made a secret society with a friend. To this day, I have never told anyone the meaning of our name 'The TTs'.)

Favoutite fight scene:
War and Peas by Michael Foreman. The animals in King Lion's country are starving but they manage to chase away the greedy Fat King and his army.

RELOADED

WHO WILL WIN?

Yishan Li

Illustrator

Favourite hero:
Spiderman

Favourite monster:
King Kong

Your weapon of choice:
A long sword

Special secret power:
Invisiblilty

Favourite fight scene:
The Spartans against the Persians in the film 300

Goodie or baddie:
A baddie with a human side

RELOADED

COMING SOON ...

MORE MONSTERS,
MORE MAGIC,
MORE MAYHEM ...

THE
DRAGON AND THE
WARLORD

BY
THOMAS BLOOR

Sheng's village is dying of thirst.
The warlord Zuko has all the power.
Sheng must find the magical dragon's pearl
to save his people.
But he's in for the shock of his life ...

Please see our website for details
www.barringtonstoke.co.uk